Night Terrors

A Collection of Short Stories

By: Dylan Gibbs

Preface

First, I'd like to start off by thanking you for choosing this book. In a world with over a hundred million books to read, somehow, we've found each other. I think it's safe to assume that you're a fan of horror, as am I, and I hope to satiate that wonderful feeling of fright you are looking for.

Although I'd love to write full-time, I am a blue-collar worker that writes when he's able. The stories in this book have been a labor of love over the course of several years. While writing the stories, I never had any intention of publishing them. Only after sharing some of the tales with family and friends, I was encouraged to do so. In short, I don't write to make money, I write because I enjoy it.

I don't know if an author is supposed to have a favorite story of their own, like a parent isn't supposed to have a favorite child. I do though, and it's "The Farmhouse." I thought back to being a child and losing a loved one for the first time. How each part of the calling hours and funeral felt like a terrifying ritual. How difficult it was to see my family in mourning. Then I thought, how can I make that experience even worse? I feel as though I accomplished the goal in the story, and I hope you enjoy reading it as much as I enjoyed writing it.

I'd also like to tell you about the story titled "Hillman House". Each of the three children in the story were named after my own three kids. I wrote this tale for them as a frightening bedtime story. Although it is a bit less gruesome than the others, I'd read through it first before sharing it with your own children. Mine seem to be way less fearful of things than I was at their age. If you deem it appropriate, I'd love for you to scare your kids, grandkids, niece, nephew, younger sibling with it.

Finally, "Gretel's Pond" is extremely meaningful to me. I originally wrote the story as a twenty-two-year-old man. Unfortunately, I had only one digital copy of the story and without getting too in-depth, it was destroyed. The story remained in my mind though and fourteen years later, I brought it back to life. It was amazing greeting my old friends and sending them back on the journey in this book. This time with better language no doubt.

I hope you thoroughly enjoy this collection of short stories, and I hope we find each other again with the next one.

Dylan Gibbs

Three Nights in Black Creek

The clock clicks over to 9:00am on the coffee machine. The water making that distinct sizzle sound as it starts to cycle through. Small puffs of steam and the smell of Folgers Dark Blend fill the air.

In the next room over Mike Otis, stirs in his bed and rubs his eyes awake.

"Mornin' Oscar," he says.

At the end of the bed, curled in most of the big blue comforter, the yellow lab picks up his head and lets out a lazy yawn.

Mike rolls out of bed and gets shakily to his feet.

"I'm getting old," he mumbles to himself.

He rubs his almost non-existent 24-year-old stomach and walks into the master bathroom.

When he finishes getting on an old pair of sweatpants and yesterday's Shins t-shirt, he reenters the bedroom to find Oscar with his head deep down into the bag of dog chow and is just crunching away.

After pouring a heaping mug of coffee, Mike makes his way over to the living room window. He pulls aside the awful, teal-colored curtains and peers out the window.

Roughly two feet of snow fell during the night and because of the snow drifting, Mike's driveway is no longer visible.

Although the air is free of falling snow at this moment, the sky is gray with clouds, ready to dump a fresh new batch at a moment's notice. The beat-up red pickup truck looks to be an island in an ocean of white, while the two old pines in the front lawn are full of glistening snow.

"Here boy! Looks like we're gonna snow blow."

Not a second before the door is opened, Oscar shoves his way past to run out into the fresh snow. He walks clumsily through the snow reaching up past his legs. Mike can't help but laugh as the old lab flips snow up into the air with his snout. Reminds him of when Oscar was just a little pup.

Mike trudges around to the back of the house in knee deep snow to the tool shed. He lifts the padlock off the catch and flings the door wide open. An old John Deere snow blower, rusted with age, sits expectantly by the door.

Mike grabs the handles and pulls it halfway out of the shed. He pushes the primer three times, pulls down the throttle and gives the pull string a hard tug. It sounds like it wants to spurt to life, but it doesn't. He travels up to the front of the snow blower to look at the rotors; they're caked with ice. He grabs a rubber mallet from the tool bench to his right and begins slamming into the ice. When the rotors feel like they have a little give, he tries again. This time when he pulls the pull string it spurts out a small puff of black smoke and kicks to life.

Mike gets about six feet out of the shed when Oscar comes hauling ass around the house. Oscar runs and jumps at the snow billowing out of the chute, trying to catch it in his mouth. He succeeds but not without becoming completely covered in snow.

"Idiot dog," Mike says, laughing.

It takes him about thirty minutes to clear his twenty-yard-long driveway. His S10 is only two-wheel drive and in this weather, it needs to be freed.

Mike brushes off the pickup truck, then brushes off old Oscar and they head into the house. A nice hot shower sounds good right about now, he thinks.

Mike gets out of the scalding hot shower and throws on a clean Pixies t-shirt and a pair of faded jeans. He walks out of the bedroom and down the hall to the study. He sits down at a large mahogany desk in front of a huge LCD computer screen. Around him are floor-to-ceiling book racks filled with his favorite literature. The section to the left of him is filled with every hard cover first edition Stephen King novel written.

Mike puts in a full day's work editing web pages. It's not his dream job but it's a steady paycheck. At least he's writing something, since writing is his passion in life.

At 5pm, he loads Oscar in the truck and pulls out of the driveway with ease. Although he lives virtually in the middle of nowhere surrounded by woods, it's only a fifteen-minute drive to his parents' house in the heart of a little town called Black Creek. Mike was invited to dinner and he's not missing a chance for a home cooked meal.

Mike pulls up to a big gray two-story house with neatly kept shrubs covered in snow all around it. First thing he sees is his tall blond sixteen-year-old sister Rachel standing on the sidewalk. She has a cell phone to her ear and looks at Mike like, "what the hell is he doing here?"

Mike opens the door to the truck and Oscar, unable to wait, jumps over his lap and onto the pavement. His tail wagging ferociously as he bounds for the front door.

"Come over and give your big brother a smooch," Mike yells.

"I'd rather not, I don't want to catch the AIDS," she replies with a grin.

"Sorry, didn't hear ya. You want to be thrown in the snowbank you said?"

"Get the hell away from me. I'm being serious," she says as he approaches.

All of a sudden, he makes a dash for Rachel, throws the petite blond girl over his shoulder and starts walking toward the road.

"Mike. Mike. MIKE!" is all she manages to say as she's tossed into the five-foot-high bank of snow.

Mike opens the door to his parents' house and unleashes Oscar to destroy his mother. Oscar flies through the living room past Mike's father and straight for the kitchen to jump on and kiss Mike's mother.

"How are the Jets doing, Pops?" he asks his dad, Richard.

Richard mumbles something completely incoherent back.

Mike rounds the corner to his parents' large kitchen and sees Oscar licking a giant bowl on the floor.

"How are you doing Mom?"

"I'm doing fine. Dinner in five."

The whole family sits down to eat around the oak dining table and Rachel starts off this evening's conversation with; "Thanks for the wet ass, it's awesome you came over."

"Watch your mouth," Richard says grumpily.

"You doing anything special tonight, Mikey?" his mom asks.

"Well actually, yeah. I'm going to see the Sad Clowns over in Oswego tonight."

"Who the heck is that?" Rachel asks.

"They're a local band. Tons of potential. They sound a lot like The Decemberists."

"Who the heck are The Decemberists?"

"You wouldn't know them; they never sang in the Mickey Mouse club."

Rachel sticks out her tongue half covered in mashed potatoes at her brother.

After the meal is complete, they all plop their dishes into the dishwasher and file into the living room together.

"Thanks for the grub, Mom. I have to get going if I'm going to catch the show in the city."

"Don't forget your damn dog," Richard says with a half grin on his face.

Mike laughs and says, "I thought he was moving in with you."

"Yeah right."

Mike pulls into his driveway to drop off Oscar before heading out to the show. He pops open the door to the S10 and steps out into the half gravel, half-snow-covered driveway. It's twilight, or close to it, and the sky is a rich dark blue. It's those brief minutes before it becomes full dark. Oscar hops down off the truck seat and walks lazily toward the steps of the front porch. Mike follows.

Suddenly there's a loud snap from just inside the woods. Mike comes to a stop and peers in that direction. He can't see anything there. From his right he hears a scratching noise and turns quickly toward the house. Oscar's pawing at the door to be let in. Mike laughs and goes up the porch steps and opens the door to the house. Oscar runs inside and Mike closes the door behind him. As he's heading back down the steps, there's another loud snap louder and closer than before. Mike breaks into a jog, jumps back in the pickup truck and slams the door. He cranks up the new Arcade Fire album and already feels silly for jogging to the truck. He backs it out of the long driveway and starts his twenty-minute drive north to Oswego.

Mike spots a car pulling out onto the street just ahead of him and only half a block from the venue. He swings into the spot and gets out; he's late to the opening band but still awhile until the Sad Clowns come on. He walks down the street to the venue, always looking at the ground, trying to avoid slipping on the icy sidewalks.

He gives his twenty bucks to a six-foot-five-inch-tall skin head bouncer who appears to be very angry about something. His hand gets a black stamp with some blurry logo on it, and he heads into the next room through big thick blue doors. The sound is the first thing that hits him. The drums are louder than anything else and the singer is barely audible, which in this case Mike thinks might be a good thing. The crowd is decent sized, probably around 350 people. Mike heads down to get a better look at things. The band isn't too horrible, but he hangs back and just kind of peers over the crowd to watch them.

The band finishes the last song of their set and announces that the Sad Clowns are up next. They begin breaking down the stage. The house lights go up a little and Mike sees her. The girl who's at almost every show he goes to. She's wearing black leather boots, a pair of nearly painted on dark blue jeans and a puffy jacket with a fur lined hood with a Ramones t-shirt. She's tall with a petite frame, and Mike stares as she flips back her shiny long black hair.

She turns towards Mike and has a look that says, "you were totally just checking me out, weren't you?"

At least she looks amused and not angry. Now that they've made eye contact for a solid five seconds or so he's got to do something. He decides to explain himself.

Mike walks over to her and says, "I'm not a creep. Just trying to figure out where I know you from."

"Yeah, that's a new line," she responds mockingly.

"No really, were you at the 'Wax Lips' show last week?"

"Of course, I remember seeing you there too actually," she says more shyly.

He catches the smell of her perfume and thinks that she smells as good as she looks.

"I love The Breeders."

For a second he's completely confused, then it hits him. He's wearing a Pixies t-shirt. The bassist for the Pixies is Kim Deal, who's also the singer for The Breeders.

"Ah, yeah. 'Cannonball' makes my top ten favorite songs for sure," he replies.

This in fact isn't true at all, but he'll say anything to remain talking to her.

The lights dim.

"Hey, I think they're starting," she says.

She grabs Mike's hand and leads him into the crowd. Her hand feels small and cold, but also soft and wonderful. He doesn't mind being led through the crowd of people one bit.

The band enters the stage, and everyone cheers. They get into position, and the singer counts to three behind the microphone. The music fills the room the singer starts wailing about being lost at sea and the deep rich lyrics make Mike start to slowly bob his head along. Between the first and second song they get the opportunity to actually learn each other's names. Hers is Lauren, and Mike of course finds it as beautiful as he finds the rest of her.

During one of the songs, she slips in front of him and leans back against his chest. He puts one hand on her waist, and they remain this way through the show, dancing, rubbing against each other, and leaning over to shout important information, like "I love this song" into each other's ears.

After the last song is over the lights kick back on and the crowd begins to disperse. Mike doesn't want the night to end here.

"Want to go get some coffee or something?" he asks nervously, looking everywhere but at her.

"You asking me or the floor? Of course I'll go with you silly."

They find a diner open just down the street a little way. They sit down in the 50's style restaurant, and both order a cappuccino and a piece of blueberry pie. They endure a little uncomfortable silence at the beginning but as more time passes, they get into talking about their jobs, families, a lot about music and various other likes and dislikes. Lauren checks her watch and realizes they've been talking for over two hours now.

"Wow, it's getting late, I'm going to have to get going in a minute."

"Oh wow, it is. Hope I can see you again soon."

"Well, I'm busy tomorrow, but Saturday looks good," she says and laughs. Saturday being the day after tomorrow.

"Sounds good to me, I'll take you out for some fine dining like tonight," he says, raising his eyebrows up and down like a goof.

"Or not. You could come see my apartment, watch a movie or something."

"Or you could come to my place, meet ol' Oscar and I could make you dinner."

"Oh yeah. That sounds great actually!" she says enthusiastically.

They exchange phone numbers and Mike walks her to her car. Before she gets in, she reaches out for a hug. Mike leans in to embrace her and she kisses him on the cheek.

"See you Saturday, Mike."

"Yea def, drive safe."

Mike just about floats to his car. He can't remember the last time he was this excited over a girl. Maybe high school, maybe never.

Mike pulls in his driveway and heads up to the house. He opens the front door.

"Pee time Oscar," he yells.

Oscar comes flying out the door, runs down the steps, then stops dead when he hits the ground. Mike lifts up an eyebrow and stares at the dog. Oscar crouches and starts to growl towards the woods. Mike takes a hard look in that direction but only sees darkness. He turns back to Oscar, who is now peeing on himself and full-out snarling.

"OSCAR! Knock it off, get inside!"

He doesn't listen, just growls and snaps wildly at the air. Mike, feeling extremely uneasy, makes his way to the dog. That breaks Oscar's concentration, he hops up on the porch and scoots into the house. Mike quickly follows.

"What the hell has gotten into you buddy?"

Mike makes his way into the bedroom and undresses down to his cotton boxers. He starts to get into bed but hesitates. He walks over and takes one last look out the bedroom window into the dark woods that surround his home. Must have been something there to get Oscar that riled up. He dismisses the thought, puts all that out of his mind, and climbs into his nice warm bed.

Mike isn't asleep for more than an hour before he sits up in bed breathing heavily. He looks around the gloomy room. His heart is pounding but he doesn't remember dreaming anything. Something else must have woken him up. Oscar lets out a low growl from the end of the bed.

Mike gives him a soft kick and says, "Quiet Oscar. Nothing's there."

As Mike lays down and settles back in, he can feel his eyes instantly start to feel heavy. Suddenly there is a chesty roar that tapers off into a horrible screeching noise from out in the woods. The volume of the sound is disturbingly loud and clear. Mike is now bolt upright in bed.

"Holy shit... holy shit. What the hell is that?"

Mike sits there breathing heavily for ten minutes that feel stretched to an hour. He hears another sound, this one a little deeper in the woods. It just sounds like a loud groan. It's definitely coming from an animal but nothing Mike has ever heard in his lifetime. It's safe to assume it's the same animal that made the roar.

The fact that the animal is moving away from the house doesn't comfort Mike much. He turns on his bedroom TV but immediately mutes it. The light provides a feeling of safety. Oscar is fast asleep and lightly snoring. A few minutes pass and Mike joins him.

Mike wakes up the same as every morning: at 9:00am with the smell of Folgers in the air. He stretches and lets out a little groan. "Mornin' handsome."

Oscar tips his head back and looks at Mike upside down with his tongue hanging out. Mike laughs.

After using the bathroom Mike pours Oscar a heaping bowl of dog chow and fills his water dish. Oscar goes right to work on devouring the mountain of brown pebbles. Mike pours himself a cup of coffee and walks to the window to take a look at the snow situation. A few sparse flakes fall here and there, but there's nothing more than a dusting on the ground. Mike makes a mental note to clear the steps off with the shovel later.

He opens the door and shouts, "Pee time Oscar!"

Oscar finishes licking his jowls and lazily trots out the front door to take care of his morning business. Usually, Mike goes and picks out his clothes and boots up the computer at this time but instead he stands by the front door in his boxers and keeps an eye on the dog. Whatever had happened late last night was already fading in Mike's mind. If he hadn't seen the TV on this morning, he probably would have convinced himself it was just a bad dream. All the same, Mike keeps an eye on the big yellow lab until he's ready to come back in.

After a hot shower and a bowl of fruity pebbles Mike goes to the study to start his editing. He remains doing so for the next six hours, stopping only once to call Lauren and reconfirm plans for tomorrow night and give her directions to his house.

After wrapping up today's work he decides to head to his local grocery store to pick up items to prepare tomorrow night's meal for Lauren. He also thinks some pizza sounds tasty and decides to pick one up on his way back. He gives Oscar a dog treat, grabs his truck keys off the end table, and steps outside. It's a lot colder out than he had expected. Mike picks up the plastic shovel that's sitting against the house and uses it to clear the wooden steps from the little snow that fell. He tosses the shovel back against the house and spins around. Something catches his eye. Just outside the woods to his right. It looks like there's a patch of pink snow.

Mike picks the shovel back up and heads toward the pink patch. He notices as he gets closer that there are some darker red spots. He uses the shovel to try and scratch off the fresh layer of snow. It's blood. There is something brown in the snow too, just a little deeper down.

Mike shoves the end of the shovel into the snow next to the brown object. He lifts the object up; it's now on the end of the shovel and he gently bounces it to shake off the snow clinging to it. He goes in for a look at the item. It's a severed rabbit's head.

Mike drops it immediately.

"Must have been some sort of dog or wolf or something that got ahold of it," he mumbles.

Chunks of it are scattered here and there just under the freshly fallen snow. It was ripped apart savagely. Mike realizes how close he is to the edge of the woods and decides he's not exactly comfortable with that, so he picks up a light jog through the snow over to his pickup truck. He starts up the quiet engine and backs the truck out of the driveway. As he heads off to the grocery store, he keeps one eye scanning the woods around his house for movement.

Mike pulls into the Walgreens parking lot and immediately sees the bright red Volkswagen Beetle in the lot straight ahead. Only one girl has that car in this tiny town and he's not too excited to see it here. He parks his truck and heads into the store. Just get in and get what you need and get right back out, he tells himself.

He manages to grab the spaghetti, the sauce, the mushrooms and the bread. When he gets to the chicken, the last item he needs, that's when he hears her voice.

"How have you been Mike?"

He turns to his left and there's Holly, his ex-girlfriend, standing there with a smile. She's dressed in black leggings, a skirt that stops just under her unmentionables and a gray sweater that hangs off one shoulder. She's your typical blond airhead with the Barbie body type.

"I'm all right, how are you?" he asks while gritting his teeth.

"I'm great. How's the job going?"

"I actually have a new job, web page design. Editing. That kind of stuff."

"Aw neat. It's been a while man. We should really get together and catch up sometime soon."

"I don't know if that's the best idea," Mike says from behind a fake smile.

"You're not still mad about the whole Brian thing, are you? That was forever ago."

He takes a deep breath and proceeds to pick out some chicken.

17

"Wow, are you really buying groceries? What's the occasion?" she asks mockingly.

"I'm making my girlfriend dinner tomorrow night."

Mike isn't sure why he said this. Perhaps because he believes Lauren actually will become his girlfriend or maybe just to see that stupid shocked expression on his ex's face. Probably the latter.

"Oh, well have fun with that," she says while slinking away.

"I plan on it."

Mike purchases the items and heads down the street to pick up a pizza. He seems to be in pretty good spirits after slaying the dragon known as Holly. He orders a double pepperoni and eats a slice while driving home. When he arrives home, he parks the car, grabs his groceries and heads for the front door. He keeps his head down, breathing out big puffs of air in the cold and walking like a man with purpose. He can't shake the feeling he's being watched from those creepy motionless woods.

Mike tosses the pizza box on the coffee table, walks to the refrigerator, tosses in the groceries and gets himself a bottle of IBC crème soda. He twists off the cap and drinks half the bottle in two long gulps. He wanders over to his DVD rack and pulls out *The Road*.

"What do you think, Oscar? Wag your tail if you want to watch *The Road*," Mike says, raising his voice a higher pitch.

Oscar immediately sits up and wags his tail.

Mike laughs, turns on the surround sound and pops in the DVD. Not only is *The Road* one of Mike's favorite books but he's watched the movie at least a dozen times since it's been out. He stares at the 52-inch LCD screen and shovels pizza into his mouth greedily. Oscar watches with hopes that some pepperoni will topple off onto the floor.

Time passes and the credits roll on the movie. Mike sits up with heavy eyes and peers over at the digital clock on the oven. It reads 9:48, usually way too early for Mike to consider bed, but with the little sleep he received the night before it sounds like a perfect time to hit the hay.

Mike strips off his clothes and tosses them into the hamper by the dresser. He hops into bed and pulls the sheets up close to his face. He closes his eyes and feels Oscar climb up onto the end of the bed.

Mike is dead asleep within a minute.

Mike sits up quickly. He heard something; he just doesn't know what it is yet. He turns to look at the alarm clock, it's 2:07AM. There is a creak and then a groan from the front porch.

"Holy shit," Mike thinks. "Someone is standing on my front porch."

His mind searches wildly for an explanation. *Maybe Holly has been drinking and came to talk. Maybe it's a stranded motorist who needs to use a phone. Only why would he just stand there? Shouldn't they knock?*

Mike clearly hears someone take two steps closer to the door.

Mike's eyes go wide.

"Aw fuck... did I lock the door?" he whispers.

He waits for what feels like an hour but is only two minutes and then slowly gets out of bed. Oscar's ears perk up, and he pays great attention to his owner. Mike's adrenaline is pumping as he brings his shaky hand up to the window shade. He slowly pulls down on the shade and peers out into the complete dark. He can't see anything at all.

Mike begins to doubt there is actually anything out there at all and thinks it's just his imagination running wild. He'll prove it to himself by flicking on the porch light.

Mike leaves the safety of his bedroom and heads into the living room toward the front door.

There's another creak followed by a loud thump of something heavy hitting the ground hard. Oscar goes crazy in the bedroom barking and snarling. Mike flicks on the porch light and opens the front door. He can't see anyone out there but what he does see sends a shiver to his very core. There is a path in the snow from his front porch to the woods.

Mike slams the front door shut and twists the dead bolt locked. He lies in bed restlessly the remainder of the night.

Mike smells the coffee brewing and knows he has to drag himself out of bed. He shuffles over to the edge of the bed and stretches.

"How did you sleep Oscar?"

The yellow lab continues laying there but his tail is thumping up and down hard against the bed. Mike uses the bathroom, fixes himself a cup of coffee and heads to the front door.

"Oscar, time to go out buddy!"

Oscar comes flying around the corner and shoots out the front door. Mike leans out the door to take a look at the tracks from last night. Between the wind and the light snowfall, he can't see much of them at all. Not even enough to tell if they are boot prints or an animal on all fours.

Oscar runs back into the house a little whiter than before he went out. It's not snowing hard but coming down steady. It's not enough to warrant a trip outside to snow blow, which is good because Mike is content with staying indoors today.

After Mike finishes his coffee, he takes a long hot shower to help wake him up. He puts on some ripped faded jeans, a brand-new black Meat Puppets t-shirt and heads out to the living room to do some cleaning. He vacuums the living room, picks up the garbage and soda cans laying around and then does a light dusting.

"There, good enough for government work. I'll just have to light some candles when she gets here," Mike mumbles to himself.

Mike heads into the study and puts in a full day's work. He stops at 5:30 so he can start making dinner. Lauren is expected at about 6pm. He puts the chicken in the oven and starts boiling the water for the pasta.

He goes over, sits on the couch and turns on the TV. Mike's stomach is in knots. After fifteen minutes pass he puts in the pasta and starts cooking up the mushrooms and the sauce.

"Actually, smelling pretty good in here Oscar, who knew?"

Mike sets the table, putting white plates and shiny silverware down on the dark brown wood.

There's a soft knock at the door. Oscar lets out a few quick barks and jogs over to see who is here. Mike's heart races as he follows Oscar's lead. He opens the front door and there she is, dark black hair flaked with snow and a very nice full-length dress jacket on. A curtain of white snow falls behind her. Mike's not sure he's seen anything more beautiful in his life.

"Hey Lauren, come on in and meet Oscar."

She steps inside the house.

"Man, it smells good in here. Hey Oscar, how you doing big guy?" she asks petting the yellow lab on the head.

Oscar is no longer wagging his tail; it's more of a full body wag at this point.

"Ha-ha, I think he likes you," Mike says.

"Wow, great place you have here."

"Let me take your coat and I'll show you around a bit," he says, extending his hand out for her coat.

Lauren slips off the jacket to reveal a sleek little black dress. Mike takes a minute to roll his tongue back inside his mouth then proceeds to take the jacket from her.

He leads her into the bedroom and says, "My master bedroom, I love it because it's got a full bath right here in it."

Next, he leads her down the hall and smirks.

"This is the main bathroom and this door on the left is a bedroom I made into a workout room. Ignore all the dust on the equipment though."

Lauren chuckles.

"And finally, here is my favorite room in the house, the study."

He swings the door open and Lauren looks around in wonder.

"This is amazing, look at all the first editions you have. Wow."

"Go ahead and take a look around, I'll go finish dinner real quick," he says, and walks out of the room toward the kitchen.

A few minutes later Mike calls to her that dinner is done and she comes out smiling.

"Chicken parmesan is my favorite," she says.

They enjoy dinner and each other's company well into the evening.

"Is it really nine already?" she asks. "It feels like I just got here".

"It really does. That's what happens when you have good company, I guess. Think you have time for a movie or do you have to get going soon?"

"Oh, I think I could make time for a movie," Lauren says, smiling.

"You can pick something out on the DVD rack if you want."

Lauren heads over to select something.

"How about *Evil Dead*? I'm feeling up for a good horror flick," she says.

"Good choice. Want a blanket for the movie?"

"Yea, but only if you'll share it with me."

She blushes a little. Mike smiles and puts in the DVD. They get wrapped up in the blanket together on the far right of the tan colored couch.

As each scary part makes its way to the screen, Lauren moves closer and closer into Mike. He reaches over to her under the blanket and holds her hand.

As the movie ends, Lauren tilts her head over to Mike and he can't help himself from kissing her. He leans in and their lips softly touch and begin to move. They stay there like that for quite some time.

When the make out session ends Lauren heads for the front door. She hesitates for a moment.

"I'd love to stay longer but it's late. I should be ladylike and head home to bed," she says with a smile.

Mike grabs her jacket and helps her get into it. Lauren leans over, gives Mike a kiss, and opens the front door.

"Oh wow, I don't think I'll be able to see in this to get home, Mike."

He looks outside and can't even see the cars in the driveway it's snowing so hard.

"You can always crash here if you want."

"Yea that's a good idea. Would you mind making up the couch for me?"

"You can just take my bed. I'll ride the couch tonight, no problem."

"I can't impose that much, please let me have the couch," she says, pouting her lips.

"Aw heck I guess so, but only because you made the face."

Mike makes up the couch with sheets and a blanket. When Lauren snuggles in for the night, he kisses her forehead and goes into his bedroom. He throws his clothes into the hamper and tucks himself in.

About half an hour later Mike hears his bedroom door creak open and soft footsteps coming toward the bed.

"Hey there, what's the matter? Can't sleep?" Mike asks the dark.

Lauren answers, "Yea, mind if I snuggle with you?"

"Come right in, warning you though that I'm just wearing my underwear," Mike replies.

"That's ok, so am I."

Lauren lifts the covers and slides on top of Mike. She lowers her face and starts kissing him. Mike puts his hands on her sides and slides them slowly down over her silky thong. They start breathing heavier and she reaches back and unsnaps her bra. He tugs at her thong; she rolls to her side and lets him pull it off her. Lauren pulls down his boxers and not a second goes by before he rolls over on top of her, entering as he does.

They make love twice and fall asleep in each other's arms.

There is a loud thud on the roof. Mike opens his eyes.

Thud.

Lauren sits up.

"What the hell was that?" she asks.

"I don't have a clue."

Bam!

The wall behind them shakes and Oscar starts barking wildly from the bedroom floor.

"What is it? What's happening?" Lauren asks with a clear panic in her voice.

"I think it's the thing from the woods. I don't know if it's a guy or an animal or what, but it's been doing crazy stuff the past couple of nights."

"Is this a prank? Something from the woods? That's made up, I know it is."

"I'm just telling you what I know," Mike says defensively.

There are loud knocks on the bedroom window, like someone rapping hard with their knuckles. Lauren screams. You can hear it run off toward the other side of the house.

BAM! BAM!

It sounds like it's slamming against the side door of the house.

"Aw fuck. This isn't good," Mike says and holds Lauren close.

She's breathing heavy and looks terrified.

The glass to the bedroom window shatters in. An arm reaches in. It's a blur in the dark but he sees it's brown. Fur? A jacket? He can't tell. Oscar snarls and jumps for the arm. He goes straight out the window with the extremity, snapping and growling.

Mike screams, "NO OSCAR!" and runs for the front door.

Lauren yells, "No Mike, don't leave me alone!" and begins to sob.

Mike can hear Oscar and the thing out in the woods. The dog barking and growling. Then that sickening roaring noise from the night before.

They're deep into the woods when Mike hears the worst sound possible. Oscar screeches, cries, then goes silent.

Mike goes and slumps next to Lauren.

"He's dead, isn't he?" she asks.

Mike's eyes fill up with tears.

He takes a deep breath and says, "When the sun comes up, I'll go find his body."

Mike tapes up the window and tells Lauren about the past two days. She sits and listens, her jaw dropping lower and lower as he goes on.

About two hours pass and it's almost full light outside.

"If I yell then call the police. Here is a knife just in case. I'm not leaving his body out there with that thing."

Lauren nods her head and takes the knife in her hand. Mike puts on a heavy jacket over yesterday's clothes and steps outside. The snow has stopped and there is a clear trail to follow. As he is about to enter the woods, Mike turns back to look at the house. There are huge stones on the roof. Those must have been the thuds he heard. He wonders what the hell could have thrown those up there.

Mike enters the woods and follows the trail. He feels more and more uncomfortable the deeper he goes. It doesn't take long before he spots the blood. He picks up his speed now that he's following a clear blood trail. Then he stops dead in his tracks. There is old Oscar slumped by a tree, covered in blood. Mike falls to his knees and just openly starts sobbing.

That's when he hears it, a small whine. Mike looks up, eyes brimming with tears and sees Oscar's head up. Oscar licks the end of his nose and puts his head back down.

"Oh my God, you're still alive!"

He runs to the dog and kisses his head. Mike scans the dog and sees a bone protruding from Oscar's side. Mike slowly puts his arms under Oscar and cradles him. He gets to his feet, takes a deep breath and starts to run as fast as he possibly can. Mike has to get Oscar to the vet, it's his only hope.

Several hours pass and Mike returns home with Lauren. They walk slowly to the porch and Mike puts his hands down on the railing. He looks straight out into the shadowy woods. A gust of wind blows back his hair.

"He's going to be fine they said, Oscar's a tough dog. He'll be back home by next weekend," Lauren says, trying to ease Mike's thoughts.

"If you're out there and you can hear me, just know next time I'll be ready. You will die!" Mike yells into the woods.

But Mike wonders if Oscar already did the job and the creature has bled to death out there. On the flip side, he also wonders if maybe it's fine. If maybe whatever that thing is, it's just inside those sinister woods right now, watching Mike... waiting.

The Farmhouse

Jake Bixby always loved his grandfather's farm. He loved the old farmhouse with its creaky floors and relics from a time long past that filled every room. Jake's fondest childhood memory was playing hide n' go seek with his cousins and Grandpa Tom. This trip was different. Jake was there for his grandfather's funeral. Many of Grandpa Tom's belongings had already been boxed up and stacked beside bookshelves and end tables. The place felt cold and empty to Jake.

"Is there something of your grandfather's that you'd like to take?" Jake's mother asked.

Jake looked around the dusty old living room.

"I don't think so," he answered. "Maybe a big pumpkin from the pumpkin patch."

Jake's mom said, "Sure, that'd be great. Do you want to wait til' your cousins get here? I bet they'll want to join you."

Jake sighed.

"Sure mom. I think I'll go for a walk down by the river for a bit first."

"Ok. But be back before dark," his mom replied.

Jake walked down the long dirt driveway and crossed the road to the other side. There was a mostly cleared dirt path that cut through a patch of woods. Jake followed this trail until he reached a stony clearing with rushing water of a small river moving past. Jake sat on a large boulder that was half in the water and began to think.

Jake was a twelve-year-old boy, tall and thin, with dark black hair swept to one side. He sat there on the rock thinking about all the times he had been to his grandfather's farm. He mostly thought about what it was going to be like the next day though. Jake had never seen a dead body before and from what his mom had told him, that's exactly what he was going to see at the calling hours the very next morning. This made Jake both sad and scared.

The light was starting to drain from the sky and Jake thought he had better get going. He hopped down from the boulder and started down the path toward the farmhouse. Something in the woods caught his eye.

"What is that?" Jake muttered to himself.

There was something glowing a greenish yellow about 40 yards into the woods. Jake began heading towards it. He stepped over fallen tree limbs and tree roots that were protruding from the ground until he reached the glowing substance. It appeared to be moss. Glowing green moss all over some rusted pipe sticking up from the ground.

"This is so cool," Jake thought. "I should bring some back with me to show mom."

Jake scooped up a large handful. It made his fingers tingle.

He made his way back down the path, occasionally looking down to see if the moss was still glowing. It was. The whole sky was a pale orange color. Jake thought he had better hurry now. It was going to be full dark soon and his mother was going to be mad. Jake began to jog.

"Oooffhh," Jake shouted as his foot caught a rock and he tumbled onto the shoulder of the road.

He lay there for a moment, stunned from the fall. His knee throbbed from where it had struck the road. His right hand felt wet and gooey. Jake looked over and his hand was on top of a dead cat. It must have been hit by a passing car some short time ago.

"Ah, sick!" Jake shouted.

Trying to hold back from throwing up, Jake began to gag. His eyes welled up as he swallowed a lump in his throat. Jake got to his feet and began thrashing his arm around spastically. He was trying to fling off the congealed blood.

After a moment had passed, Jake looked down at the mangled cat. It was an adult, all black, with its side split open. Its back legs looked to be at a wrong angle. There was some of Jake's moss on the cat's stomach. The rest of the moss was on the road. Jake bent over and scooped it up. There was miraculously no blood on it. Jake stuffed it into his pocket and began to cross the street.

"Mrrrrawr."

Jake spun on his heels and stared at the cat.

"MRRRRAWR!"

Jake couldn't believe his eyes. The cat was standing up. It was looking straight at Jake. It leaped across the road into his grandfather's field. He could see the glow of the moss, still on the cat, fading as it got further and further away. It vanished into the night.

Jake saw a white SUV in the driveway as he made his way up to the farmhouse. His Aunt Jen had made it, which meant his cousins would be inside. Jake ran up the old wooden steps to the porch, and the front door flew open.

"Where the hell have you been!?" his mother shouted from the doorway.

"Well... uhh.. there was this cat... and uhh," Jake stuttered.

"It doesn't matter. Get in the house and go wash up for dinner. It's already getting cold," she scolded.

Jake walked into the living room and went up the stairs to the bathroom. He could hear the clinking of the silverware on plates as people quietly ate in the kitchen below. Jake stared down at the sink drain, watching the dark red blood swirl around as he washed his hands.

"That cat was dead," he thought. "There's no way it just got up and ran. It makes no sense."

Maybe the cat had only been injured and it ran off to die somewhere else. Jake didn't think that had been the case though. He shuddered thinking about how cold that blood felt on his hand.

Jake sat down at the dinner table across from his cousins. Erica had dark black hair like Jake. She was thirteen, a year older than Jake, but in the 8th grade just like he was. Erica's little brother was eight years old and had hair so blond it was almost white. His name is William, but everyone called him Billy.

"Why are you both wearing overalls?" Jake asked with a smile on his face. "Are you planning on milking some cows?"

Jake felt his mother's hand slap the back of his head almost immediately. That made the whole family laugh.

"Hey Jake. After dinner do you want to pick some pumpkins?" Billy asked excitedly.

"No. After dinner is bed," Aunt Jen answered. "We need to be up early for the calling hours."

"Maybe we can go out tomorrow after that," said Jake.

That night Jake, Erica, and Billy were all in an upstairs bedroom together. There were three twin sized beds all in a row. At the end, closest to the door, was Billy already fast asleep. Erica and Jake were whispering back and forth in the dark. They talked about their grandfather, they talked about how nervous they were to go to the funeral home, and they talked about Jake's experience with the cat.

"You think that moss brought the cat back to life?" Erica asked.

"Honestly, I hadn't thought about that," answered Jake. "But that sounds pretty impossible, right?"

"Yeah, it does," said Erica. "Glowing moss sounds pretty impossible as well. Maybe you can show me tomorrow."

Jake jumped to his feet.

"I can show you right now."

Jake grabbed his pants from the floor and reached into his pocket. He yanked out a handful of moss. Only to find it didn't give off any light. It didn't glow at all; it was just a clump of plain old moss. Erica saw the look of disappointment on Jake's face.

"I believe you Jake. We should get some sleep though," Erica said.

Soon they were fast asleep.

The next morning, Jake's father picked him and his mother up and drove them to the funeral home. Jake had never seen his dad in a suit before. He thought he looked pretty cool. Jake recognized some faces around the room but mostly everyone was a stranger to him. The room was full of chairs and even had some couches. On the far side of the room was a shiny wooden casket with the top half open. Jake could see his grandfather's bushy white beard from the door. He got the sudden urge to hide behind his father.

"We'll go up there when you're ready to," Jake's father told him. "Go hang out with your cousins for a bit and I'll come check on you later."

Jake went over to an old blue couch and sat down next to Erica. Billy was sitting on the floor playing with some monsters filled with goo.

"Have you gone up there yet?" Jake asked, peering over at the casket.

"No, we got here right before you did," Erica answered.

Some guy that called himself Uncle Hank came over and asked them what grade they were in now. Jake was pretty sure he didn't have an Uncle Hank though and just stared quietly at the floor.

Some time passed and Jake's father came to get him.

"Looks like it's about time for us to go up there, kiddo," he said.

Jake was reluctant but followed his dad. Jake noticed a wooden step stool in front of the casket. He had seen other people kneel on it but Jake stepped right on top of it to get a better view inside. His mother and father were beside him. Jake could hear his mother starting to cry. Grampa Tom was his mom's father. Jake noticed his grandfather looked a little strange. He was wearing makeup and there was no hat on his head. Grandpa Tom always wore a hat. Jake's mother whispered something to her father, began crying harder, and stepped away from the casket. Jake's father followed her and embraced her in a hug. Jake turned back toward the casket, pulled a wad of moss from his pocket and quickly shoved it under his grandfather's back. Jake stood there staring at his grandfather for two minutes straight. When nothing happened, Jake sighed and walked back over to Erica.

"Guess it's not magic moss after all," Jake said.

Erica's eyes were puffy like she had just finished crying. She shrugged and forced a little smile.

"It was worth a try," she said.

The following day was going to be the funeral followed by the burial and Jake was not looking forward to it. However, the calling hours had ended. Jake and his cousins raced up the old farmhouse stairs and changed into play clothes. Jake's father had brought them all out to the barn and given them a rusty wheelbarrow to bring out to the pumpkin patch.

"Get me a tall one," Jake's dad told him.

The kids were running off toward the pumpkins.

"You got it dude!" Jake yelled back.

A couple of minutes later they arrived.

"Holy crap, there's got to be a hundred pumpkins," said Billy.

"I think there's even more than that," said Erica.

Jake began stepping over giant green leaves and vines to look for the very best pumpkins to carve. He pulled out a small jack-knife and cut one free.

"This one is perfect for Dad," he shouted.

The children began filling up the wheelbarrow one by one.

"Mrrrrawr."

Jake stopped dead in his tracks and looked over at Erica.

"Did you hear that?" he asked.

"You think it's the same cat? There's got to be a dozen barn cats around here," Erica said.

Then they saw it. Sitting on top of a rather large pumpkin was this glowing green thing that was once a cat. You could see some patches of black fur poking out from the moss but just barely. There was way more moss on it than the night before.

"Hissssss!"

"Billy, get behind me," ordered Jake.

It was too late. The second Billy went to move the cat pounced on his back.

"MRRRAWR," it roared as it slashed at Billy's back.

Erica grabbed a large stick from the ground and swung it straight into the cat. The cat went flying through the air. It hit the ground on all fours and immediately started running at Jake. Jake, still holding the knife, instinctively stuck it out in defense.

"MRRRAWR," the cat howled as it slammed into Jake.

The knife went firmly into the cat's throat.

"Hissssss."

The cat, covered in moss, stood there in front of Jake. It stared directly into his eyes for what felt like an eternity. Then the cat turned and ran off through the field. Jake could still see the knife lodged in its neck as it raced through the pumpkin patch and out of sight.

"Welp... do you believe me now?" asked Jake.

"I always believed you. I'm very scared Jake. Can we please get out of here?" Erica asked.

Jake turned and looked at Billy. The back of his shirt was in shreds, but he only had a few scratches that were deep enough to bleed.

"Get in the wheelbarrow Billy," Jake ordered.

With a small wince, Billy hopped on to the pile of pumpkins. Both Jake and Erica had to push but they made short work of it, fearing that the cat would return.

When they got back to the farmhouse the kids ran inside to tell their parents what had happened.

"Dad... DAD! You'll never believe what happened," Jake shouted.

"SHHH," his dad said sternly.

The look on his dad's face, Jake could tell something was wrong. Jake could hear his mother on the phone with someone in the kitchen. His Aunt Jen was crying loudly.

"I don't know how the hell something like this could happen. Yes... We'll meet the police there. We'll be there as soon as we can."

Jake's mother hung up the phone.

"We've got to go now guys," Jake's mother told the other adults.

"Jake, you and your cousins go watch some TV. We'll be back as soon as we can," Jake's father told him.

"What's going on dad?" he asked.

"I'll let you know when we get back. We don't have a lot of information yet," his dad replied.

The three children sat on the couch. The light from the TV flickered throughout the living room as the skies outside the farmhouse grew dark around them.

BAM!!

The front door to the house flew open and smashed into the wall. A dark shape stepped into the door frame. It was an old man with a bald head and huge puffy white beard wearing a suit. He had glowing greenish-yellow moss all over his back and shoulders. It was Jake's grandfather.

"HIDE AND GO SEEK LITTLE ONES," the thing bellowed.

Jake stood up and looked at the creature that had once been his grandfather. One eyelid seemed to be ripped open and the other completely shut. Its lips looked terrible.

"Did they sew them shut when you die?" he wondered.

It lurched toward the children with its hands outstretched. It was baring its teeth and making some kind of gurgling noise. Billy was the first to scream but not the last. The three of them raced up the stairs and down the hall.

Thump... Thump... Thump

That thing was coming up the stairs. Erica dove into the bedroom closet. Jake dropped to the floor and rolled under the bed. Billy was running from one side of the room to the other until he finally jumped into a cardboard box. He pulled the flaps down over his head.

Thump... Thump

That thing had reached the top of the stairs. Jake listened quietly to see if it was coming his way.

"OLLY OLLY OXEN FREE," the thing shouted from the hallway.

Nobody moved. Jake was breathing so heavily that he was sure the creature would find him first.

BAM... BAM

It was punching holes in the hallway walls. You could hear the drywall clattering to the floor each time it pulled its fist out. Jake could see the bedroom door from under the bed. He saw it open and his grandfather's dress shoes taking steps into the room. The glow from the moss was making the whole room an eerie green color.

"Please don't hurt me Grandpa Tom," Billy said from inside the box.

The creature began to laugh. It was a deep hoarse laugh that sounded nothing like their grandfather.

Billy began to scream as the creature lifted the box high into the air and threw it into the hallway. Billy lay there half out of the box, books all around him, not moving. Jake felt a sudden surge of adrenaline hit him like never before. He rolled out from beneath the bed and stood up.

"You're not my grandpa!" Jake shouted.

It looked at him with its solid black eye and a hideous grin. Erica burst from the closet and threw a baseball bat to Jake. Jake caught it out of the air and swung as hard as he could into the creature's head. The creature smashed into the wall and fell against the bedside table. It made a terrible hissing sound and bared its teeth at Jake. Erica rounded the bed and threw a golf club at the creature. She missed and smashed out half the window next to the bed.

The creature seemed to be glowing brighter and stood up. It was laughing louder and louder. It picked up the bedside table and flung it with ease into Erica. It smashed into her chest and knocked her to the ground. Jake swung the bat again, but the creature caught it out of the air. With all his might, Jake jumped and kicked the creature square in the chest. It fell back into the window and the broken glass sliced right through its neck. The head tumbled out the window and the body fell to the floor. Jake stared at the body, waiting for it to move. It remained still.

Jake walked over to Erica to help her up when she yelled "Billy!"

Billy was getting up from the pile of books. All three of them embraced in a hug. Erica was crying, they all were.

Over the next few days, the kids talked to a lot of police officers and men in suits. Jake showed them where the moss grew and guys in hazmat suits were all over the woods. Helicopters were flying overhead, landing and taking off again. Everyone assured Jake that it was all over with and that he was safe now. He couldn't shake the feeling that that wasn't true. What about the cat with a knife in its neck? What about Billy and the moss growing out of those scratches on his back?

A Dead Man's Journal

October 3rd, 2013, 0900:

I bought this journal to document a trip I'm about to take. My buddy Tim overheard some old-timers talking about some ghost town. Apparently, it's in the middle of a national forest and thought it'd be a hoot if we went on a hike to check it out. Tim is one of those larger-than-life personalities that loves to tell stories you can't believe. I'd say about 90 percent of the time he's full of shit to be exact. Since he was in a tackle shop when he got the details, I'm inclined to believe this is going to be part of that 90%. He had these guys mark the location on an old paper map. My girlfriend Sam has wanted to go hiking, so naturally it's turned into a couples thing once I told her about it. Tim is bringing his girlfriend Jackie along as well.

I bought an engagement ring for Sam last weekend. When I find the right moment on this trip, I think I'm going to propose. I've never met anyone like her in my life and I hope she'll say yes. Anyway, our packs are full and we're ready for an adventure. We leave tomorrow.

October 4th, 2013, 1200:

We have been hiking for about 3 hours. The ladies wanted to stop for a lunch and to rest up a little. None of us have any kind of hiking experience and I certainly feel like I should have broken in my boots better before leaving. My feet are killing me already and I'm pretty sure I have a bruise on my side from this stupid pack digging into me. Tim showed me on the map where we are heading and I brought it up on google maps on my cell phone. You literally can't see anything. When you zoom into the area everything is blurred out. Sam tried on her phone and it's the same thing. Strange.

October 4th, 2013, 1830:

We are making camp. The sun sets around 7pm and we didn't want to get caught trying to put up tents in the dark. Tim is hacking at trees with a hatchet he brought to get us some firewood. Should I tell him there are thousands of dry sticks and tree limbs on the ground everywhere? We've been on a well-worn trail up until the last hour of our journey. I was nervous to step off the path and start heading into the unknown but I think with modern technology it's pretty hard to be lost anywhere. We'll probably get to this ghost town and they'll have a gift shop with t-shirts for sale... if it exists at all.

October 5th, 2013, 0800:

Holy crap it was cold last night, I could barely sleep in that damn tent. Also, I think every animal in the forest came to check out the fire before it died out. All around us we heard things walking around and darting off. It gave me the creeps. I think we've decided to spend the night in one of the old ghost town houses tonight, if they're truly there. Walls should prove to have better insulation than these super thin tents. Tim thinks we'll get there in about 5 hours. If the forest gets thicker, it's going to take a lot longer though. Also, I forgot to bring anything to shave with and my face is all stubble. I hope Sam digs the mountain man look.

October 5th, 2013, 1600:

I can't believe we actually made it. This place is not at all what I pictured. First, we were greeted with was a sign stating, "RESTRICTED AREA. NO TRESPASSING BEYOND THIS POINT. ENTRY PROHIBITED BY THE UNITED STATES GOVERNMENT." We of course ignored this sign all together and walked right through a downed section of metal fencing. Second, it appears to be military housing. There are two cabins full of metal frame beds with old mattresses, two cabins with no windows and locked doors, and then a huge cafeteria building. The buildings don't look modern, maybe this place is from the 80s or

90s? My guess is that it used to be used for military training, but that probably hasn't been the case for several years now. The odd thing is, there are badge readers on the locked cabins and they are lit up red. How is there power to them all the way out here? Also, there are surveillance cameras on each of the buildings and even two on the fences, I wonder if they are being monitored somewhere. If they are, I'm sure we'll find out soon enough. I think we'll look around some more and see if we can't figure out what this place was.

October 6th, 2013, 0100:

The rest of the day was wild. Sam and Jackie were outside the fence getting firewood and they discovered a body. Sam came back shaking and crying, it really rattled her to find something like that. Tim and I followed the girls back out there to check it out. It was immediately obvious to us it was a soldier. They had been wearing boots, camo pants, a tan colored shirt and camo jacket. There was no body per say, it was mostly just a skeleton. I thought it may be fake at first because the clothes look to be in decent shape in comparison with the body. I did a search on google, which took almost 20 minutes to get a damn signal, and it said that's common. Apparently, a person left outside can decompose down to just bones in 9 days if it's summer and there are plenty of insects. I don't know if this guy died five years ago or two months ago. Either way, we have a duty to report this when we get home.

The other thing is, we searched this guy's pockets and found a keycard stating, "Level 3 Access". We brought it back to the two cabins that had badge readers on them. The first reader made a beep and the light stayed red. The second one turned green, and the door clicked open. Jackie said she heard the surveillance camera move but I think it was just her nerves. Tim and I went in first. The first thing we noticed was the weapons. There were handguns, shotguns, rifles, and boxes upon boxes of ammunition. The gun racks looked to be about a third of the way full, room for a lot more to be stored. There were also huge maps of the woods with things circled in red. The maps were in front of a long table and chairs. In the back of the cabin there was an office. I tried the drawers and one of them slid open. There was a red folder that read "Confidential US Military Documents. Contents must be destroyed after reading.", which struck me as something you'd see in a James Bond film, not in real life. The folder was empty but on the tab on the inside it said "Operation: Grey Man". Tim has been going off about that all night, he's going wild with theories. They were up to something out here.

Well, everyone has been asleep for a while now. We slept inside the cabin with the beds. Somehow the lights work out here, and none of these bulbs are out. I'm starting to think this place isn't as old as I originally thought.

October 6th, 2013, 2100:

This morning Tim and I decided to take a better look at the map inside of the keycard cabin. I guess we were thinking that if we found a dead body out here, maybe there are clues to what happened at one of the sites circled in red. There are 5 areas circled in total. Tim was particularly interested in going north to check out a cave. I absolutely hate caves and would have a full-blown panic attack going inside of one, so I picked a site south to check out. Tim thought we should take weapons with us, just in case. I didn't feel comfortable taking weapons from a military base, but Tim talked me into it. I just took a small 9mm handgun and Tim took some absurdly large automatic rifle. We grabbed our ladies and some essentials and split up.

Sam and I reached our area quickly, it was maybe an hour's hike. The trees opened to a little meadow with a stream running through it. It would have been picturesque if there weren't bullet casings everywhere. There had to be thousands of them. I assume this was used as some sort of range for target shooting. I didn't see any targets up or any trees that had been hit hundreds of times but why else would there be so many casings? We took some pictures with our cell phones to show Tim and Jackie later and then we hiked back to the cabins. On our way back we heard gun shots in the distance. I assume it was Tim, there's no way he takes a gun out to the woods and doesn't fire it.

Still, I tried to call his phone to make sure everything was all right. I had enough service to call but it went right to voicemail. I left a message to call me back.

That was about five hours ago. It's pitch black out now and Tim and Jackie are still out in the woods somewhere. I know they didn't bring their tent or sleeping bags. I hope Tim was smart enough to bring some flashlights and matches. Sam suggested we go look for them but it's such a bad idea to wander around the woods at night. They probably lost track of time and didn't want to hike back in the dark themselves. We'll head out in the morning and see if we can find their trail.

October 7th, 2013, 1200:

When Sam and I got up this morning, we packed up some first aid items and left the cabin in search of Tim and Jackie. We got about three steps out the door and noticed one of the other cabin doors were open. It happened to be the cabin that was previously locked with the badge reader that we couldn't get into. My very first thought was that Tim found another keycard out there and he was exploring the cabin. Sam and I ran up to the cabin and threw our packs down against the wall. The badge reader on the outside of the door was green. When we went inside, I couldn't believe what I was seeing. It wasn't a cabin at all, it was an elevator. The room was completely empty other than a freight elevator in the center with blue railings all around it. It had a single panel in the corner with a green button, red button and a small keyhole.

Sam and I discussed it for a moment, then decided to climb into the elevator and press the red button. Nothing happened. Then I tried the green one. The elevator started to rattle and we went down. It felt like a long distance but I have no way to know how deep we traveled. When the elevator hit the bottom floor, the smell hit us like a ton of bricks. I fought hard not to throw up but lost the battle. Sam held her composure but not without pulling her shirt up over her nose. The elevator led out into a hallway with white floors and walls. There were people lying dead all over. People's torsos were ripped open, some people were torn completely in half, I even saw someone missing a head. Down the hallway walls you could see four giant gashes where something was dragged. The bodies near the elevator were all wearing military uniforms, but as you traveled down the hallway it changed to bodies in lab coats. They weren't like the skeleton in the woods, these still had flesh and looked mostly like people still.

We went from room to room to search for Tim and Jackie. Most rooms held huge stainless-steel tables with hospital equipment inside. Some rooms had supplies like oxygen tanks and the biggest CT scanner I've ever seen. Every step I took, I knocked bullet casings around by my feet. Something had gone horribly wrong down there.

When we found no trace of Tim and Jackie, we took the elevator back to the surface. We needed some fresh air and to clear our heads. I called 911 on my phone and got through to an operator. I explained that my friends were missing in the woods and that there were dead bodies out here in the cabins. The operator asked for my latitude and longitude, and I gave them to her off my phone's GPS. Her voice got real stern and she asked me to repeat them. I did and then there was an audible click. It seemed like I was hung up on. I called back several times and each time it rang and then clicked dead. I have no idea if they're sending anyone.

I told Sam it's time for us to get out of here. We're going to head north and see if there's any sign of Tim. I'm packing up all our belongings and we're hiking out of these woods tonight.

October 7th, 2013, 1800:

Sam and I hiked north for about an hour and a half. We found the opening to the cave, I took a flashlight from my pack and shined it in. I could see Tim's legs sticking out from behind a large rock about 150 feet into the cave. I shouted at first but Tim wasn't moving. I gathered as much courage as I could and made my way into the cave. Sam was right behind me, holding onto the back of my shirt to help steady herself. When I reached Tim, I broke down in tears. It was Tim's legs all right, but that's all it was. Tim's torso was missing completely. That's when we heard it. An ungodly roar from further down, followed by the meaty slaps of bare feet on the floor of the cave rushing toward us.

I ran as fast as I could and made it to the cave's entrance but Sam wasn't with me. I screamed for her to run but she just stood there frozen. I pulled my handgun from my bag and aimed it into the darkness. I pleaded with Sam to move. It was too late. This monstrous thing emerged and just slapped Sam into the cave wall. I saw blood go everywhere. It kept heading right for me. It looked like a muscular man with a long white beard and sickly yellow eyes. It had grey cracked skin like a rhino or an elephant and was completely naked. It had to be eight feet tall and hands so big they looked like claws. I don't know how I know this, I guess it's just a gut feeling, but it's ancient. It's like it's the oldest living thing on earth.

I aimed center mass and began to fire rounds into the thing's chest. It just kept walking toward me. I don't think the bullets penetrated its skin. When I knew that I couldn't stop it with the gun, I turned on my heels and broke into a run. When I tell you I ran, I mean I ran for my life. I never looked over my shoulder to see if it was following me, I just tore through the woods. Which brings me to now. I am deep in the woods and completely lost. I can't get a signal on my phone. It's about to get dark. I'm going to set up my tent here and sleep over night. Hopefully tomorrow I can get a signal and find my way out of here.

I can't believe they are all dead. Poor Sam. I'm going to miss you so much.

October 8th, 2013, 0200:

I'm in my tent, writing this by flashlight. I didn't light a fire; I was afraid that thing would find me. I know it's still out there. I heard it earlier, deeper in the woods screeching as it searched for me. I'm shaking so bad I can barely write. I've never been so scared in my life.

Wait. I think I just heard footsteps. Is it my imagination or is that thing out there?

My God. I hear something breathing on the other side of the tent.

Hillman House

The smell of baking cookies fills Abe's nose as he stares out the living room window. He sees autumn leaves swirling and skidding across the front lawn. Abe's not looking for leaves though, he's looking for the first sign of trick-or-treaters. It's Halloween night and the first year Abe's parents are letting him go out without adult supervision.

Abe is a twelve-year-old boy, thin and tall. He has a mop of blond hair and is wearing an oversized ghostbusters flight suit. His father enters the living room blasting the monster mash song on his cell phone.

"It's about that time. Want me to help you get your proton pack on?" his father asks.

Abe's father had bought him an expensive proton pack from Spirit Halloween that has sound and it lights up.

"Heck yeah," he answers. "Eli should be here any minute."

There's a knock at the door.

"Right on time!" Abe shouts.

The front door creaks open and a redheaded twelve-year-old boy with freckles pokes his head in.

"You ready to bust some ghosts or what?" he asks.

"Let's roll out," Abe answers.

Abe picks up a pillowcase off the arm of the couch and charges out the front door. Eli is wearing the same ghostbuster flight suit as Abe. The proton pack is the only difference. Eli is wearing a blue old school Kenner pack. They jump down the cement steps and walk over to the sidewalk.

"Let's head down to Willow Street and cross to Oak," Abe says.

Oak Street is the most popular street in town on Halloween. The folks that live there have money and often give out a handful of candy at a time or even full-sized candy bars.

"After we hit Oak, are we going straight over to the Hillman place?" Eli asks.

"Yeah, if you don't chicken out," Abe answers.

The boys trick-or-treat at each house on Willow Street. They pause here and there to admire the scary lawn decorations or a particularly interesting jack-o'-lantern.

They get to the corner of Willow and Oak and hear a little girl crying. First, they spot a green pumpkin bucket on its side with candy spilling out. Then they see a young girl lying on the sidewalk holding her face.

"Hey, what's wrong?" Eli asks.

The young girl turns her head to reveal bloody scabs all over the right side of her face. Her right eye is out of the socket and dangling down by her cheek.

"I was hit by a car," she yells.

The boys start to panic.

"I'll stay here with her. You run back to that house and tell them to call 911," Abe orders.

Eli turns and starts to jog when he hears laughter. He stops and turns around. The girl is rolling around on the sidewalk, holding her side and laughing as hard as she can.

"You guys will fall for anything," she says through heavy breathing.

Now the boys recognize her. It's a girl from their class named Gina. She is always pulling pranks on the boys.

"I bought one of those latex scar kits off amazon. Not bad, eh?" she asks while pushing her candy back into the pumpkin bucket.

"You scared me half to death," Eli says.

"You guys hitting Oak Street? I'll join ya," says Gina.

"Yeah, but you might want to split after that. We're going to knock at old man Hillman's door after we're done with Oak," Abe says with a smile.

"You idiots have a death wish?" asks Gina. "You do know he is an actual vampire, right? He only comes out at night. You always see bats flying out of that creepy old house. Plus, I heard he keeps a coffin in the basement and sleeps in it during the day."

"You don't have to go if you don't want to, but me and Eli are knocking on that door and becoming legends tonight," Abe says.

Eli yells, "Who ya gonna call? Ghostbusters!"

The three kids start heading down Oak Street in search of the best candy of the night.

Three houses in and the kids reach a house with a fog machine and a bunch of older teenagers in costumes passing out candy.

Eli hesitates and says, "Maybe we should skip this one."

"How are you going to go up to the Hillman place if can't go up to some teens?" asks Gina with a grin.

"Yeah man. I've heard he's an actual serial killer. My uncle said Hillman murdered a bunch of women and children in the 70s and 80s and was arrested for it. They blew the trial somehow and he got off on a technicality. He is extremely dangerous and might be abducting people to this day," Abe tells Eli.

"Well hell, if we're knocking on that dude's door, he better have those berry skittles. Those are my favorite," Eli says laughing.

All three of the kids are laughing and head up to the teenagers to get their treats. There's fog rolling over the front lawn from a fog machine by the porch steps. They can hear screams and rattling chains coming from a speaker on the porch railing. A teenager dressed as Jason Vorhees tells them their costumes look awesome and passes out a handful of candy. After each of them receive their candy, the teenager dressed as Michael Myers begins fast walking straight toward them to scare them off the lawn. It works. The kids go running across the street to the next house.

The kids are halfway done with Oak Street and Abe stops to admire a huge jack-o'-lantern. Someone had stuck hundreds of toothpicks coming out of the pumpkin's carved mouth, making it look like some sort of demented scarecrow.

"Holy crap this is cool looking," says Abe.

Eli wasn't looking at the pumpkin. He was staring down the street. From here the kids can see the turn onto the dead-end road and the thought of knocking on the door to the Hillman house loomed ever closer.

"I've never heard that story about him being a vampire before," Eli says still staring down the street. "I heard that old man Hillman died when we were little. People see him from the road, walking past his windows and moving about the house. He never leaves though because he's a ghost. He haunts anyone who dares step onto his property."

Gina shrugs.

"Ghost, serial killer, vampire. Whatever he is will be terrifying, and tonight we find out just what that is."

The kids finish trick-or-treating Oak Street. Their pillowcases are already a quarter full of candy; they heave them over their shoulders and turn onto the dead-end road. It doesn't help their nerves that two of the streetlights are out and the road is darker than it should be. They pay no mind and walk a short distance to the end of the road.

The house looks haunted. It's old and missing paint. Some of the shutters have fallen off or hanging askew. The grass around the place hasn't been mowed in ages, it's up to the children's knees. There is a single bulb glowing a soft yellow on the porch. Two of the windows are lit up; one upstairs and one downstairs near the front door. The kids look at each other to see if anyone is going to bail. No one does. They walk through the lawn and go up onto the creaking old porch. Abe lifts his fist and slams it into the front door. He knocks three times and then waits. They can hear movement inside.

A lock clicks and the door starts to open. A fuzzy black and white cat slips out from behind the door and starts to rub the children's ankles, purring loudly as it does.

"Panda, don't you go running off now. You hear me cat?" a voice says from behind the door.

The door opens the rest of the way to reveal a rather average looking old man. He's wearing overalls and a white shirt with a mustard stain on the front.

"Well, I'll be. I don't get many trick-or-treaters these days," says Mr. Hillman. "I did pick up some candy just in case though."

Mr. Hillman tosses a full-sized bag of M&Ms into each of their bags. The kids thank the old man, and they hop down off the porch.

Abe starts laughing first, then Eli, then Gina.

"I can't believe we've been afraid of that guy our whole childhood," says Abe.

"Yeah, he actually seems like a really nice guy," says Eli.

Gina shrugs.

"So, what street do you guys want to hit now?"

The kids walk down the dead-end road and back onto Oak Street. Old man Hillman watches them from the front doorway until they're out of sight. He closes the door and picks up a sharp knife from the table. He lifts the blade to his face and licks blood from its serrated edge. Hillman turns and walks into a dark room where a woman starts to scream.

Gretel's Pond

"Hey Ron, time to get up buddy," his father calls from the hallway.

Ron's eyes begin to open. He looks to his left at the alarm clock on the nightstand. It's 5:32am. Ron groans loudly and rolls out of bed. Today is a special day for Ron. His father, Hank, is taking him fishing for the first time. Ron is a ten-year-old boy with dark shaggy hair and dark eyes. He's a bit short for his age and a little chubby, his mom says he's husky. Ron hears the roar of an engine from the garage. His father started the truck; he better get moving. Ron throws on his jeans and yesterday's Nike t-shirt and jogs out to the truck. Hank is throwing fishing gear into the back of the truck.

"Some donuts in there and a couple of bottles of o-jay," Hank tells Ron.

Ron hops up into the passenger seat and eyes the box of Entenmann's donuts. He grabs a chocolate. His father sits down beside him, snatches a powdered donut for himself and backs out of the driveway.

After about 25 minutes of driving, they pull off the road and onto a dirt path. Ron notices half a dozen signs to keep out and warnings of contaminated water.

"Hey, isn't this Lily Pond?" Ron asks. "We can't fish here. This is where they had that chemical spill and made all the fish poisonous."

"No son. That's a story they came up with to deter people from coming out here. There ain't an ounce of truth to it," says Hank.

They park the truck and step out near the shoreline. The pond is massive. It's about 4 miles long and 3 miles wide in a near perfect oval shape. There's a small island in the northern section. The pond connects to a major lake via a channel on the northern end as well. There are camps and summer homes over on the lakeside but almost nothing on the pond, aside from a few run-down cabins on the south end.

The guys grab an old wooden rowboat from against a tree and move it to the water's edge.

"My dad left this boat here Ron. Our family has been using it for 30 years," says Hank.

"Yeah, I can tell," laughs Ron.

They fill the boat with a tackle box and a couple fishing poles. Hank grabs some newer looking oars from the bed of the truck and Ron climbs into the boat. Hank shoves the boat into the water and leaps on, causing the tiny boat to violently rock from side to side. Hank sits down, puts the oars into place and begins rowing them out to deeper water.

The sun is just starting to come up, giving everything that early morning glow of orange. There's a light fog on the water, mostly around the edges of the shore. Ron and Hank can hear teenagers somewhere to their south but can't see a boat. Sound on the water is tricky, it can sound like someone is right next to you and they're miles away. Hank has rowed their little boat out to the middle of the pond now.

"Well Ron, it's about time I told you why we're out here," says Hank.

"What do you mean? I thought we came to fish," replies Ron.

"We will, but first I want to show you something. My father brought me out here when I was a kid to show me and his father brought him," says Hank. "I want you to watch the water beneath the boat carefully. She'll show herself pretty quickly, she always does."

Ron looks around but only sees the dark water, smooth as glass. He sees the occasional disturbance of a fish jumping close to the shore. A water bug is making its way across the surface, close to the boat. Nothing unusual at all.

Five minutes pass and Ron sees something in the distance. Something under the surface of the water is causing a wake behind it and it's heading in their direction. Ron turns and looks fearfully at his father. Hank reassures him with a little smile.

"I've never seen her tip a boat or hurt a soul. You're perfectly safe son," Hank says.

The wake reaches the boat, and Ron sees what appears to be giant dark green stone tiles gliding underneath their tiny vessel. He notices them covered with algae, with deep grooves running through them. Ron's mind searches to make sense of the situation. He notices a curved edge to the tiles and finally a massive webbed paw with long thin claws pushing through the water. Ron whirls around and stares his father in the eyes. Hank is bald with a long grey beard and a face full of wrinkles. His light blue eyes meet Ron's.

"Dad," Ron says. "Is that a turtle?"

Hank laughs.

"That's Gretel. She's the biggest turtle on the planet from all accounts. People from these parts have been keeping her a secret for at least a hundred years."

"How can a turtle get that big? It's the size of a house," Ron asks.

"No one knows. Best we can tell Gretel's a type of snapping turtle. She measures about 20 feet long. The fish get into the pond from the lake, they come in from the channel, and she eats her fill. People have seen her grab birds right off the surface as well," explains Hank.

The wake from the massive turtle comes to a stop and the water starts to spin. Gretel makes another pass by the boat, and the guys can see her in better detail. She raises her large head and exposes a beak like mouth. Her huge eye seems to watch them as she soars by.

"Has Gretel ever eaten a person before?" Ron asks nervously.

"Of course there have been stories over the years, but I don't think any of them are real. That being said, I don't think I'd go swimming in Gretel's pond," answers Hank.

Ron starts laughing.

"What did you guys name the other turtle?" Ron asks while pointing beyond his father's back.

Hank spins around and stares at an even larger wake moving toward them. Hank stands up, making the little boat sway. His face is serious now. His eyes are darting around trying to locate Gretel. He spots her wake moving south toward the sound of the teenagers. The teens are out in a small boat themselves now. Hank looks back at the massive dark shape moving beneath the water. The new turtle seems to be at least 5 feet longer. Hank slams back down into the seated position and picks up the paddles. He begins to row.

"In all my years, I've never seen a second one," Hank shouts at Ron. "I'm sure it's friendly but we're going to play things safe and get to shore."

Hank's effort is wasted as the new turtle reaches them in no time. A huge greyish-green head rises from the water with a wide-open beak of a mouth. In a quick motion, the turtle bites the side of boat. Wood splinters apart and flies everywhere. Hank falls backwards into the water, his hand clutching to the end of the boat as he falls. Ron falls out on the opposite side and starts frantically splashing around. Water gets into his mouth, and he swallows it down coughing. Ron's flight response kicks in, he flips to his stomach and starts to swim. He's not a strong swimmer but knows enough to tilt his head to the side to suck in air as he goes. He kicks hard and starts to make distance from the shattered boat.

Hank looks around, holding a big chunk of the boat to keep him afloat. He doesn't see the turtle or his son.

"RON! RON! SHOUT TO ME SON," Hank screams.

Hank listens but hears no response. He does however hear the thrum of an outboard motor. The sound is getting closer and closer.

"Hey mister! Climb in," someone shouts from behind Hank.

Hank spins around to see two pimple faced teenagers glaring at him with fear in their eyes. Hank swings around and grabs onto the side of their boat. The two boys help pull him in. A teenage wearing a black hat with orange hair poking out around it slams the little motor into full throttle and sends them straight for shore.

"No, no! We've got to turn around. My boy is still out there," says Hank.

"Sorry mister, we didn't see any boy and we ain't getting killed by Bowser today," the teen replies.

Ron feels sand beneath his feet and stops swimming. He stands up and starts to run for shore in the waist high water. It's hard work and Ron collapses on the sandy beach. He turns and looks for the wreckage. He can see some debris but not well. Ron hopes his father has also made it to shore. Something is off though; there is still water to his right and to his left. Ron stands up.

"Oh no, oh no," Ron says. "I'm not on the main shore. I swam to the island."

Ron looks around. The island is small. You can walk across it in two minutes or less. There are several trees and a bunch of dune grass. On the right side of the island the sand is all dug up. Ron walks over to take a look. All over the place are half buried giant white golf balls. Only these are way too huge to be golf balls and they are all broken. Ron leans down to feel one.

"Oh man, I think these are turtle eggs. They're as big as I am," exclaims Ron.

SPLASH! A huge turtle erupts from the water and climbs onto the shore near Ron. It's walking quickly toward him with its head outstretched. Ron runs to the nearest tree and begins to climb. The tree is young; the branches can't hold his weight and snap off as Ron climbs. The turtle reaches the base of the tree and raises its head. It begins snapping wildly at Ron's feet.

Hank quickly thanks the boys for rescuing him and takes off in their boat toward the wreckage. Hank looks to his left and sees Gretel soaring along beside him. She's very interested in the fast-moving vessel. Hank slows to a stop around the floating wood that was once his family's boat. He doesn't see Ron anywhere.

"The island is closer than shore. Maybe he swam there," Hank thinks to himself.

Hank starts moving quickly toward the island and immediately sees his boy in a dire situation. The colossal turtle the teens called Bowser was outstretched and snapping at Ron up in in a tree. Ron did not look high enough.

With complete disregard for his own safety, Hank let the boat slam onto the shore of the island and leaps out. He begins running straight at the turtle. Still to his left, Gretel also launches herself onto the shore and moves quickly by Hank's side. Gretel passes Hank and slams into Bowser. She opens her giant beak and latches onto the side of Bowser's head. Gretel shakes hard and pulls away a chunk of Bowser's face and his entire left eye. The turtle flinches away from Gretel and moves quickly back into the water. Bowser's wake is heading straight for the channel into the lake.

"You're a hero Gretel," Hank laughs with relief. "Come on down Ron, I think we're safe now."

Ron jumps from the tree onto Gretel's hard shell and then jumps again into the sand. Hank runs to Ron and embraces him with a hug. Gretel slips back into the dark cold water of the pond.

"Thank God you're safe," says Hank. "Maybe we don't tell your mother that a giant turtle almost ate you."

Ron laughs.

They return the boat to the teenagers, who in turn give them a ride across the pond to where their truck is parked. Hank thanks them again for their help and watches as they speed off toward the south end of the pond.

Ron hears some movement as they walk up to the truck. A six-foot-long turtle slides into the water from shore.

"I don't think Gretel's pond will stay a secret for much longer dad," says Ron.

"What makes you say that?" Hank asks, staring at the same spot in the pond as Ron.

"Because over 20 giant turtle eggs hatched on that island," answers Ron.

Hank turns and stares Ron in the eyes, "What the hell did you just say?"

Dear Reader,

I appreciate your support with my books tremendously. If you enjoyed the book and you'd like to help me further, please consider leaving a rating or review. Either one of those on Amazon or Goodreads will help others find and select my books for purchase. That small act would mean the world to me. Thank you!

-Dylan

Other books by Dylan Gibbs

From the Woods
A Collection of Short Stories

Demon Twins
(Book of Demons #1)
A Novel

Demon Blade
(Book of Demons #2)
A Novel

Summer of Shadows
A Novel

Phantom Rift
A Novella

Dylan Gibbs is from a small town in Central New York. He is a family man first and foremost. He has a wonderful wife and three beautiful children. Although he works a blue-collar job, he's spent his adulthood writing stories. Dylan has always been curious about the things that frighten us most. His writing style is primarily geared for young adult readers but anyone with a love of horror and thriller genres will enjoy. He has plans for several future publications.